Prince Nautilus

To Stephanie - L.K.M.

To Annelise and Verner - H.S.

Prince Nautilus

LAURA KRAUSS MELMED
HENRI SORENSEN

The illustrations in this book were done in acrylic paint on watercolor paper. The display type was set in Rundfunk. The text type was set in Novarese Medium. Color separations by The Colotone Group. Printed by Kingsport. Production supervision by Linda Palladino. Designed by Robin Ballard.

Library of Congress Cataloging in Publication Data

Melmed, Laura. Prince Nautilus / by Laura Krauss Melmed ; illustrated by Henri Sorensen.   p.   cm. Summary: A fisherman's two daughters, one vain and lazy, the other generous and brave, set out to help a prince who has been imprisoned in a seashell. ISBN 0-688-04566-9.—ISBN 0-688-04567-7 (lib. bdg.) [1. Fairy tales.]   I. Sorensen, Henri, ill.   II. Title.   PZ8.M5214Pr 1994 [E]—dc20 93-37432 CIP AC

LOTHROP, LEE & SHEPARD BOOKS • NEW YORK

In a weathered shack by a windswept shore, two poor girls lived with their father.

The older sister, named Columbine, was a great beauty, but her heart was as cold as kelp. Though the girls' mother had died years before, Columbine never lifted a finger to help at home. Instead, she gossiped in the village, or preened before her looking glass, yearning for a wealthy husband who would shower her with gold and jewels.

The younger sister, Fiona, was kind and capable. Each day she swept the floor spotless. Each night she had the stew pot bubbling when her father returned with his fishing nets.

After her morning chores were done, Fiona walked by the edge of the sea. Her hair whipping wild in the wind, she gazed out at the horizon, imagining what lay beyond it.

One day as Fiona stood daydreaming, a large seashell washed onto the shore. The perfect milk-white spiral filled her hands, its lip glowing as pink as dawn. She raised it to her ear to hear the echo of the sea. Instead, she heard a voice crying, "Help me, help me, please!"

Alarmed, Fiona dropped the shell, then knelt on the sand beside it. "Who are you?" she whispered.

"I am Prince Nautilus," the voice replied. "An evil sorcerer has shrunk me to the size of a minnow and trapped me in this shell. Here I've lived, tossed by wind and waves, until a lucky tide washed me to your feet. Please! Help me to break the evil spell and return to my father's kingdom!"

Fiona ran home. "Listen!" she cried, and held the shell to Columbine's ear.

When Prince Nautilus had repeated his tale, the sisters exclaimed, "We will help you!" But though Fiona spoke from the goodness of her heart, Columbine had her own plans. When the prince was free, she thought, he would not be able to resist her beauty. Someday she might be queen!

Prince Nautilus said that at daybreak he would guide the sisters to a magic isle where the spell could be broken.

The next morning, Fiona filled a jug with fresh water and wrapped two oatcakes. For good luck, she tucked her mother's precious lace handkerchief into her pocket.

The sisters carried the seashell to the end of the jetty. There, at the prince's urging, they called out three times: "Swan-of-the-Sea, hurry to me."

Instantly, a battered old dory appeared before them. "Climb aboard," said the prince. "Swan-of-the-Sea will point the way while you row. The spell must be broken before nightfall, when the magic isle slips beneath the sea."

Fiona took up the oars, rowing with all her might.

As the boat followed the rising sun, flashes of colored light skipped over the swells. Soon, hundreds of little rainbow-striped fish leaped and frolicked around the dory.

"How beautiful you are," murmured Fiona.

Suddenly, a jet of murky water shot sky-high, then fell back to reveal a huge fish. Its whiskery face was encrusted with barnacles. Its mouth glittered with row upon row of sharp yellow teeth, which it gnashed with an awful grinding sound as it plowed toward the rainbow fish.

"Row faster!" shrieked Columbine. Instead, Fiona quickly emptied her jug, then refilled it with seawater, letting the rainbow fish rush in to safety. Somehow, hundreds seemed to fit.

As the monster reached the boat, the last little fish wriggled into the jug. The creature plunged beneath the surface with a loud slap of its tail.

"How dare you, Fiona!" yelled Columbine. "You've wasted our drinking water. Pour those stupid fish back at once!"

Fiona held the jug close.

Columbine grabbed the oars and rowed angrily. Suddenly, shrill cries rang out overhead, where two seabirds battled in a flurry of beating wings. One bird, larger than the other, was trying to pull a herring from the smaller one's mouth. With a piercing squawk, the attacker jabbed viciously, then snatched the prize. The injured bird fell into the dory.

Fiona quickly bound the lace handkerchief around the bird's bloodstained wing.

"Get rid of it!" cried Columbine, and she lifted an oar to frighten the bird away.

But at that moment, a pale pink mist appeared in the distance. "Prince Nautilus, I see a mountain!" exclaimed Columbine, dropping the oar overboard in surprise.

"That is the magic isle," said Nautilus. "We must get there before sunset."

But with only one oar, the sisters could not row forward. Swan-of-the-Sea could only turn 'round and 'round in circles.

"We're stranded!" cried Columbine. "We'll die of thirst!"

With a little pop, one rainbow fish jumped from the mouth of the jug into the sea. Out leaped another and another and another. The little fish laid themselves head to tail, forming a bridge to the isle, and a silvery chorus sang out, "Walk on our backs, Fiona!"

"Thank you," said Fiona, "but Columbine must come with me." Then, taking her sister by the hand, she led her over the sparkling rainbow bridge. Behind them, the seabird flew off as Swan-of-the-Sea disappeared.

When they reached the shore, Prince Nautilus said, "On the far side of the island lies a bottle-green lagoon. If we reach it before sunset, we can break the sorcerer's spell forever."

As the prince spoke, a sad wail rose up over the rocky beach. From behind the boulders came a mournful song:

"Oh, woe is me, woe is me,
I long to swim the salty sea,
to ride the waves,
to rock to sleep,
cradled in the inky deep.
Oh, woe is me, woe is me,
the sea shall see no more of me."

Fiona ran to the rocks. There lay a giant sea turtle, its eyes glistening with tears. One leathery flipper was wedged fast between two stones.

Though Fiona pushed and pulled until her arms ached, the heavy boulders would not budge.

"Hurry up, Fiona!" Columbine called.

Fiona remembered the prince's warning. "We must go, Turtle. I hope this bit of food gives you strength to pull free!" She crumbled an oatcake on the sand. The turtle nibbled feebly.

"What about me?" whined Columbine. She grabbed the second oatcake and gobbled it up. Fiona said nothing, but set off along the ragged coast. Columbine dragged behind, complaining with every step.

The slippery rocks seemed endless, and the girls soon grew exhausted. Columbine sat down, refusing to go further.

Fiona sank to her knees. Tears rolled from her eyes. As they slid into the sea, a great, hulking shape lumbered out from the surf. It was the turtle.

"Kind girl, your food gave me strength to free myself. Climb onto my back and I'll carry you to the lagoon."

Fiona was grateful, but once again she refused to leave Columbine. So the turtle carried both of them to a sparkling green inlet nestled in a curve of golden sand like an emerald in a royal crown.

"The sun is sinking!" cried Fiona, scrambling down.

"Quick!" said Prince Nautilus. "Throw the shell into the water, as far as you can."

Columbine snatched the shell and tossed it out. It fell close to shore and returned on the next wave. Then Fiona, with an arm toughened by years of scrubbing and hauling, heaved the shell to the center of the lagoon. It sank for a moment, then bobbed up.

The water began to churn and bubble. A foaming geyser erupted, spewing out the monstrous fish. With an awful roar, the creature opened its dripping jaws to crunch the shell between its jagged teeth. The girls cried out.

Then the seabird appeared, holding the handkerchief, the lace again as bright as new snow. Flying above the terrible creature, the bird dropped the bit of cloth down onto its back. Instantly, the handkerchief spread into a huge net, entangling the scaly beast. Though it thrashed and twisted, lashing its powerful body from side to side, the more it struggled, the tighter the net drew. As the setting sun touched the water, the monster fish stilled and sank beneath the surface of the lagoon.

The water returned to its former calm. The sisters, straining to catch a glimpse of the shell, jumped at the sound of footsteps behind them. They turned to see a young man approaching, the seashell in his hand.

"Prince Nautilus!" cried Columbine, smoothing her hair. The prince bowed to her handsomely, then turned to Fiona. Locked in his lonely prison, he had fallen in love with the brave and generous girl. He took her hand and asked her to marry him.

Fiona smiled and spoke softly. "Prince Nautilus, I cannot marry you now. For years I have longed to see the wide world and its wonders. After this taste of adventure, I am hungry for more!"

No sooner had she said this than Swan-of-the-Sea appeared. Before their eyes the dory was transformed into a magnificent sailing ship. The little rainbow fish became a crew of hardy sailors, the turtle a fit ship's captain, and the seabird a fine first mate.

They sailed home, where Fiona embraced her father and took him aboard the ship. Kind Prince Nautilus invited Columbine to come as well. But that night as they lay anchored, Columbine stole away with a sack of the ship's gold, and they never saw her again.

The next morning at sunrise, Swan-of-the-Sea carried Prince Nautilus, Fiona, the old fisherman, and
their loyal crew away toward the shining horizon.
In search of bold adventure
the little group set sail
and what they found
would quite astound—
but that's another tale!